I0648261

Thomas Hutchinson

Jolts and Jingles

A Book of Poems for Young People

Thomas Hutchinson

Jolts and Jingles
A Book of Poems for Young People

ISBN/EAN: 9783337206529

Printed in Europe, USA, Canada, Australia, Japan

Cover: Foto ©Andreas Hilbeck / pixelio.de

More available books at **www.hansebooks.com**

JOLTS AND JINGLES

A BOOK OF POEMS

FOR YOUNG PEOPLE

BY

THOMAS HUTCHINSON

———

*Sing on! sing on! let the dull world
grow young.*

—THE BURDEN OF ITYS.

———

LONDON

STANESBY & CO. 179 SLOANE STREET S.W.

(FORMERLY MURRAY & STANESBY)

DERBY AND NOTTINGHAM

FRANK MURRAY

1889

JOLTS AND JINGLES

BY THE SAME AUTHOR.

———

AN ESSAY ON THE LIFE AND GENIUS
OF ROBERT BURNS: 1887.

(Out of print)

———

BALLADES AND OTHER RHYMES OF A
COUNTRY BOOKWORM: 1888.

(Also out of print).

———

FIRESIDE FLITTINGS: A BOOK OF
HOMELY ESSAYS.

(In preparation).

———

A DREAM OF SHELLEY, AND OTHER
POEMS.

(Also in preparation.)

JOLTS AND JINGLES

A BOOK OF POEMS

FOR YOUNG PEOPLE

BY

THOMAS HUTCHINSON

———

*Sing on! sing on! let the dull world
grow young.*

—THE BURDEN OF ITYS.

———

LONDON

STANESBY & CO. 179 SLOANE STREET S.W.

(FORMERLY MURRAY & STANESBY)

DERBY AND NOTTINGHAM
FRANK MURRAY

1889

TO OSCAR WILDE

To you who wrote THE HAPPY PRINCE,
   The sweetest tale of modern times,
In individual gratitude
For hours of tearful happiness
   I dedicate these Children's Rhymes.

CONTENTS.

JOLTS AND JINGLES.

A

Thank goodness, we sha'n't have to study and stammer
Over Latin, and sums, and that nasty French grammar ;
Lectures, and classes, and lessons are done,
And now we'll have nothing but frolic and fun.

—ELIZA COOK.

LIZZIE.

Seldom, seldom are earth's creatures
Bless'd with such angelic features,
As is Lizzie, aged seven,
Truly fashioned she in Heaven.

Gay as summer is she ever,
For a moment quiet never:
Like a billow of the ocean,
Always in perpetual motion ;
Hither, thither, like a feather
Blown about in windy weather.

Bright as sunlight in the daytime ;
Blithe as mower in the haytime ;
Or as lark, in mid air winging,
Its glad song of praises singing ;
Or as bee in sunny hours
Sipping sweets from fragrant flowers.

Sweetest music Lizzie's voice is—
How the soul at it rejoices,
Palpitates the heart, and flutters
At each syllable she utters :
How she prattles, how she chatters,
Wise in the abstrusest matters.

Yet with all is she in favour ;
In their love for her none waver ;
Father, mother, sisters, brothers,
And a hundred hundred others—
Such as uncles, aunts, and cousins—
Flock around her in the dozens ;
Crying, as they crowd about her,
Earth would dreary be without her

WAKE UP, LITTLE BOYS AND GIRLS.

Wake up, little boys and girls,
  'Tis time to be out of bed,
Enjoying the morning breeze
  Before its freshness has fled :
The sun is beginning to shine,
  And bright beams abound in the East ;
Wake up, little boys and girls,
  Astir are both bird and beast.

Wake up, little boys and girls,
  The lark is soaring on high,
And pours forth such melody,
  As wafts e'en *our* souls to the sky ;
And hundreds of songsters more
  Are sounding their Maker's praise ;
Wake up, little boys and girls,
  And join in their joyous lays.

Wake up, little boys and girls,
    And away to the fields, away ;
The daisies are wide-awake,
    For rose they with dawn of day ;
The lilies unfold their leaves
    Of spotless, snow-like white ;
Wake up, little boys and girls,
    And enjoy the glorious sight.

Wake up, little boys and girls,
    The sluggard alone would sleep—
Alone, on a summer's morn,
    His head 'neath the bedclothes keep :
There's health in the morning breeze,
    There's joy in the birds' sweet strains ;
Wake up, little boys and girls,
    And join in the glad refrains.

THE TEACHER'S ADDRESS ON EXAMINATION DAY.

Silence in school, the inspector is coming,
   Whate'er else you do you must not make a noise,
Nor murmur at tasks, like a lot of bees humming,
   Silence in school—don't you hear me, you boys ?
Hands on your heads, by your sides, mind, you'll rue it,
   And badly, I promise, if you don't obey ;
Hands on your heads—yes, I thought you could do it,
   Shoulders, fold arms, behind backs—that's the way.

Silence in school—chattering cease—oh ! my goodness,
   Who would believe what a teacher must bear ?
Silence in school, let me have no more rudeness,
   Do as you're bid, or—do, Robert, take care.
Hands up, down, out, in, up, down, up, down, oh !
     murder,
   That all are asleep an onlooker would say ;
Now listen again, if you please, to the order—
   Hands up, out, in, down—well, at last, that's the way.

Silence in school, the inspector's fast nearing ;
   You must do all that you can while he's here,
To win his good grace by your gentlemanly bearing,
   Heads up, shoulders back, now true boys you appear.
Don't be afraid when you give him an answer,
   Speak out like men, let him hear what you say ;
Arms folded, behind—little faster there, Dan, sir,
   Left turn, right about, as at first—that's the way.

Silence in school, keep your tongues and feet quiet ;
   What ! must you shuffle about on the floor ?
Mark time, one, two, one—but without such a riot,
   Step softly, one, two—halt, that's worse than before.
Try it again, now ; yes, that's a bit better ;
   Think what you're after, 'tis all I need say,
When you do your dictation, or are writing your letter,
   Softer, one, two, one, two, one—that's the way.

Silence in school, the inspector's approaching,
   But don't start to shake when you see him come in,
Keep up your hearts, for you'll get no more coaching,
   And don't get excited or make such a din.
A teacher's life's nothing but examinations,
   No wonder his hair oft ere manhood turns grey,
Who else could put up with his petty vexations ?
   Out, in, up, down, front, prepare, sit—that's the way.

Silence in school, I can't bear such a clamour,
　　Listen to me, one more hint I will give :—
Don't be in a hurry to finish your grammar,
　　Or you'll all be failures as sure as you live.
Silence in school, at the door's the inspector,
　　All your best manners must you now display ;
Silence in school, heads erect, James, erecter,
　　Attention, fold arms, well done, boys—that's the way.

LITTLE MISS MOFFITT'S BIG DOLL.

Little Miss Moffitt
  Has a big doll :
Boys, do not scoff it,
  For have you not all
Something or other
  That plays the same part ?—
Now, Joe, do not bother
  To hide your toy-cart :
Your pop-gun, dear Billy,
  Don't pop up your sleeve :
And Neddy, 'tis silly
  Your soldiers to leave.

Little Miss Moffitt
  Has a big doll,
And that she does love it
  Proof is not small :—
To bed she does take it,
  And lies, oh ! so still,

For fear she should wake it
　Or do it some ill :
And when, in the morning,
　She rises refresh'd,
Despite Sammy's scorning,
　She clasps it to her breast.

Little Miss Moffitt
　Has a big doll,
And tho' the paint's off it,
　And it looks quite droll,
Yet—in her eyes—it
　Equall'd was ne'er :
Tho' *you* would despise it,
　What need *she* care ?
'Tis still her dear dolly
　Whose cheeks once were bright,
And sparkling as holly
　On Boxing Night.

WHY KATE'S MAMMA LOVES CARLO.

You ask me, my dears, why I love Carlo so?
I thought you the reason had learnt long ago;
But, since what I thought has turned out to be wrong,
The tale now I'll tell if you'll sing me a song.

You see little Kate, there, so lovely and fair,
With bright Saxon eyes and as bright flaxen hair;
'Tis on her account that I love Carlo so,
As I really expected you knew long ago.

One day she and I—she was scarce two years old—
Were walking beside where a great river roll'd,
And Carlo was with us, dear Carlo, so true—
Yes, doggie, you know we are talking of you.

Well, Carlo and Kate began romping about,
When all in a moment I heard a loud shout:
Oh! what was my horror, on turning around,
To see in the river Kate fast being drown'd.

I screamed and I shrieked, yet how helpless was I ;
Ah ! little I deem'd that assistance was nigh,
Till Carlo sprang in and my darling did save
From an early and sudden and watery grave.

Now need you not wonder, my dears, any longer
That for Carlo my love seems each day to grow stronger :
And to give him three cheers you will own can't be
    wrong,
Nor to sing me for telling the tale a nice song.

'TIS BETTER TO LAUGH THAN TO CRY.

This wide world of ours is full of fair flowers,
  Tho' oft when sharp showers come pattering down,
Drooping and pining till again the sun's shining
  Them see we—divining they like not Heav'n's frown :
Not more so do we, and far rather would be
  Where folk never see over-clouded the sky,
Yet still when it rains, tho' our pleasures are pains,
   'Tis better to laugh than to cry.

In ages long sped, as perhaps you have read,
  Or, it may be, heard said, two philosophers dwelt,
One of whom ever wept—save, of course, when he slept—
  Laughing aye t'other kept, so light-hearted he felt :
Now, as everyone knows, the former of those
  Died not until close ninety years had passed by ;
But the latter lived on till a hundred were gone—
   'Tis better to laugh than to cry.

So tho' trouble and care you are fated to bear—
　And this is not rare—at your lot look not glum ;
Nor shed coward tears e'en when sorrow appears,
　Or your soul's fill'd with fears of woes yet to come :
Avaunt all your sadness, worse is it than madness
　To drive away gladness and blubber or sigh :
Save dotards none do so :—tho' shipwreck'd like Crusoe,
　'Tis better to laugh than to cry.

THE DUCK THAT CRIED QUACK, QUACK.

THERE WAS ONCE a little duck that was wont to cry
  Quack, Quack,
Whenever drops of rain pattered down upon its back ;
Yet it did not quack for sorrow, for its heart was filled
  with glee,
And it did not quack for anger, for more pleased could
  duck not be.

It waddled hither, thither, quacking, quacking all the
  time,
To the rhythym of the raindrops in its great joy adding
  rhyme,
For it cared not for fair weather or a clear unclouded sky,
But it loved each silvery raindrop as a boy loves apple pie.

It was not afraid of catching cold at all, at all, at all,
For it knew that not a raindrop that upon its back should
  fall
Would remain a single second or besmear a single feather,
And so nothing did it hate so much as warm, sunshiny
  weather.

Thus was it that this little duck was wont to cry Quack,
  Quack,
Whenever drops of rain pattered down upon its back,
For it did not quack for sorrow, for its heart was filled
  with glee,
And it did not quack for anger, for more pleased could
  duck not be.

PAPER, PEN, AND INK.

Whilst writing a short letter to a friend the other day,
   I was very much surprised to hear Paper, Pen, and Ink
Engage in conversation. and much eagerness display
     To prove which in the eyes of man serves him the
      most, I think.

The Paper was the first that spoke ; said he, "You'll
     both agree
     That I to man am of more use than either of you two ;
I carry all his messages across both land and sea,
     And, in return, the secrets of his heart he lets me
      view."

" Ha, ha," laughed Ink, "you needn't brag, for what
     would be your use
     If aught the current of my love for you should chance
      to stem ?
'Tis I that into your dull mind man's messages infuse,
     'Tis only when *I* am with you that you can carry them."

The Paper gave a scornful laugh, and cleaied his voice to
    speak,
But just then in an angry tone the Pen put in his
    word ;
"Dear friends," he said, " tho' I do not to quarrel with
    you seek,
Still can I not help feeling grieved at what I just have
    heard.

" You talk as though you did not know 'tis only by my
    aid
That either of you is of any value to mankind ;
Men send their messages in words, by me the words are
    made,
So that in me of all us three the greatest use they find."

They then began to wrangle so, and raise so loud a noise,
That I their conversation was unable to make out,
For like three gossiping old dames, or three light-hearted
    boys,
They, each of them, at the same time, did to the
    others shout.

Yet, notwithstanding this great din which so my ears
    annoy'd,
I could distinguish some few words pitched in a louder
    key ;

Of these, "Parchment" and "Pencil" were most fre-
    quently employ'd,
  Tho' uttered in a different tone of voice by all the three.

The noise at last became so great that I all patience lost,
    And dash'd the Pen into the Ink with such force that
      it broke,
  This, too, upset the Ink across the Paper, which I toss'd
  Into the fire, and all again was quiet—*then I woke.*

CHARADE.

My first invites all people to quit their wicked ways,
And, underneath its steeple, unite in prayer and praise,
For e'en the worst of mortals may have their sins forgiven,
And sometimes thro' its portals is found the road to
      Heaven :
But oh ! the woe and sorrow oft theirs who turn away,
And put off till to-morrow the duties of to-day.

My second leads to glory, to death, howe'er, as well ;
Delights in onslaught gory, and makes of earth a hell ;
Brings tears and tribulation to many a cheerful hearth,
And, with loud exultation, to carnage issues forth :
Yet with loud shouts of gladness its advent oft is hail'd,
Altho' with sighs of sadness ere long as oft bewail'd.

My third the dwelling-place is of many a mighty king,
Endow'd with all the graces of which the poets sing—
Majestic, gentle, stately, yet in the bloodiest fray
By all his foes fear'd greatly—so enter ne'er, I pray ;
For, should its lord and master be anywhere about,
Afraid of dire disaster, how fast would you rush out !

My whole oft in the church is our alms soliciting,
As oft, too, in the porch is doing the self-same thing :
Yet, at the Easter season, be he or saint or sinner,
He ne'er knows a good reason to shun a vestry dinner ;
Still, let us not begrudge him the dainties he devours,
But 'neath the fifth rib nudge him, and wish that they
    were ours.

SANTA CLAUS.

Who has not heard of Santa Claus,
Child-loving, child-beloved Santa Claus,
Wonder-working Santa Claus?

He visits the earth at Christmas time,
When the joy-bells merrily, soothingly chime,
And fill men's hearts with peace sublime.

He comes in the dark, for he loves not the light,
He loves not the day, so he comes thro' the night,
When the stars in the heavens are shining bright.

By mortal eye he never was seen,
Tho' in hut and in hall he often has been,
In castle and royal palace, e'en.

On Christmas morn, when girls and boys
Jump out of bed with laughter and noise,
How their eyes are gladden'd with heaps of toys!

Their stockings are full, and their boots full, too,
Of soldiers with coats of every hue—
Red, yellow and black, white, orange and blue :

Of rosy-cheeked dollies with golden hair,
Of horses with manes flowing free and fair,
Of painted balls to throw high in the air—
How they wonder who ever has put them there !

Perhaps papa, or perhaps mamma,
But papa and mamma only gaze in awe,
With the puzzledst look you ever saw :

Till at last papa, after a long, long pause,
Suddenly cries, " They are there because
Good children are loved by Santa Claus."

Thanks, Santa Claus, for each goodly present,
To little prince, and peer, and peasant,
For thou helpest, indeed, to make life pleasant.

MARGUERETTE'S LETTER TO MAUD.

DEAREST MAUD,—
You'll remember you asked me
   To tell you, in rhyme if I could,
The news of the day, as editors say,
   When beneath the old oak-tree we stood,
On the morn that our holidays came to an end,
And to school once again we our ways had to wend.

Ah me ! dearest Maud, I have puzzled
   My brain, I am sure, twenty times,
In trying to find what, maybe, to your mind
   Are the simplest and readiest of rhymes :
For—till now, I confess, I did not at all know it—
It's *such* a hard task to be aught of a poet.

Last Tuesday we had a grand party—
   Miss Morgan was married, you know—

And we danced until ten, and, dear Maud, even then
  Did to bed most unwillingly go :
And I dreamt the whole night about dances and dancers,
Mazurkas and polkas, Caledonians and Lancers.

On Thursday Miss Morgan's successor
  Her duties began, and we think,
To judge from her manner—and, mind you, we scan her—
  From loving her we need not shrink :
She wears a brown dress, and her jacket's brown, too ;
Her hair is jet black, and her eyes are dark blue.

Dearest Maud, I had tooth-ache on Friday,
  Yet the girls simply smiled at my pain,
Tho', to tell the truth, I more inclined was to cry—
  Now I am all better again :
Aunt Mary to see me on Saturday came,
What a pity it is dear old auntie's so lame.

I'm working quite hard at my French now,
  For papa says he'll take me to France,
If the language, Maud dear, I can speak by next year,
  So, of course, I must not lose the chance.
What fun it will be among French folks to roam,
How nice for a while to make Paris one's home.

There are lots of things more I've to tell,
   Had I only the time so to do,
But the tea-bell is ringing, so I must be bringing
   To an end my rhymed letter to you :
So, with love, dearest Maud,

          I am yours,

             MARGUERETTE.

P.S.—I hope soon a *long* answer to get.

JACK FROST'S FROLIC.

Jack Frost " one morning sprang up from sleep,"
While the wakeful stars still their vigils did keep,
And he cried aloud that, ere earth was awake,
A holiday scamper o'er it he would take :
Then away from his home in the icy North
Southward he merrily bounded forth ;
       But, so noiseless his tread
       As onward he sped,
Men slept just as soundly as ever they slept
Ere out of the cold Arctic Regions he stepp'd.

O'er the hedges and trees, as he rapidly pass'd,
The brightest of diamonds and pearls he cast,
That a sparkle as clear as the stars o'erhead had ;
And the fields in a mantle of silver he clad :
The housetops, too, of both village and town
He crown'd—one and all—with a lily-like crown ;
       And the window-panes
       In the streets and lanes
He adorn'd with pictures of fern and flower,
To gladden man's heart at daybreak's dull hour.

The ponds in jackets of mail he array'd,
And the babbling brooks in their courses stay'd,
That in warm sheets of ice he might them enfold,
To protect pike and trout from the winter's cold :
Eastward and westward his footsteps he bent,
Leaving his impress wherever he went,

  And when morning broke,

  And mankind awoke,

They knew right well who amongst them had
  been—

All nature inlaying with glorious sheen.

A REAL CHRISTMAS STORY.

" *Tiss me, unkey, 'tause it's Tissmass,*"
    Little Lizzie cried to me,
    As she sat upon my knee ;
So I press'd her to my bosom,
And I kiss'd her three times over,
    And she clapp'd her hands with glee.

" Tell me, unkey, a tue 'tory,"
    And she kiss'd me thrice again—
    Gave me kisses, eight, nine, ten ;
So I told her of the tidings,
Told her of the glorious tidings :—
    " Peace on earth, good will to men."

Told her how the angels sang them
    To the shepherds while men slept,
    To the shepherds as they kept

Vigil o'er their flocks at midnight ;
Told her how all hearts with gladness
    At the glorious tidings leapt.

Then I told her of the Infant
    In the stable lowly born,
    On the earliest Christmas morn ;
Told her of the loving Saviour
Crucified by Pontius Pilate
    'Twixt two thieves, and crown'd in scorn.

Told her, then, how He o'ercame Death ;
    How on the third day He rose,
    And until the fortieth's close
Was again on earth a dweller,
How He then to heaven ascended,
Angel-guided, white-apparell'd,
Seen alone by the Apostles
    Whom to do His work He chose.

Then I told her how for our sakes
    He had lived and He had died,
    For our sakes was crucified,
How His death brings life eternal :
Told her how He intercedes still
    For us at His Father's side.

" Tank oo, unkey, for the 'tory,'
   Little Lizzie sweetly said,
   And she slowly raised her head,
And she gave me six more kisses :
Then her mother gently whisper'd
It was time good little maidens
   Soundly were asleep in bed.

LITTLE MILLY'S TEN TO-DAY.

Little Milly's ten to-day,
  Let us trill a roundelay,
  As we gaily laugh and play,
Little Milly's ten to-day.

Quickly time does pass away,
  Little Milly's ten to-day,
  Maiden Milly, joyous, gay,
Quickly time does pass away.

Little Milly's ten to-day,
  Happy, heedless, bright-eyed fay,
  On her lips smiles ever play,
Little Milly's ten to-day.

Merry as the month of May,
  O'er the meadows she does stray,
  Maiden Milly, joyous, gay,
Merry as the month of May.
                  C

Little Milly's ten to-day,
    Happy, heedless, bright-eyed fay,
    Let us trill a roundelay,
Little Milly's ten to-day.

HALF-AN-HOUR IN THE NURSERY.

(*Enter* MARIA, FANNY, *and* NED.)

MAR. How cold it is, how loud the North wind blows,
　　　How cutting is the air ; alas for those
　　　Who have, like us, no nice warm winter clothes !
FAN. Or blazing fire at which to toast their toes.
NED. Or watchful friends to rub their freezing nose.
MAR. Fie, Master Ned, to jest at others' woes.

NED. *(singing).* Little Jack Horner
　　　　　Sat in a corner,
　　　　Eyeing his Christmas pie ;
　　　　　He put in his thumb
　　　　　And pulled out a plum,
　　　And cried, "What a *bad* boy am I !"

Enter ANNIE *(crying).*

MAR. What ! crying, Annie?　What's the matter, dear ?
　　　Come here and tell your sister,

And let her wipe away each naughty tear
   For fear—.

NED.   The "black man" kissed her.

MAR. Don't heed him, Annie, he's a wicked boy
   His little sister to annoy.

NED. *(singing).* If I had a donkey, and he would
          not go,
   Do you think I would beat him? Oh, no, no:
   I'd pat him on the back and cry, "Gee-woa."

FANNY *pats* NED *on the back and cries* "*Gee-woa.*"

NED.   Hee-haw, hee-haw,
   The wisest donkey you ever saw
   Is crying now, "Hee-haw, hee-haw."

MAR. That's right, dear Ned, for once you've told the
          truth.

FAN. Hee-haw, hee-haw, you are a noble youth.

NED. *(singing).* There was once a wee maiden called
          Annie
   Had two sisters, Maria and Fanny,
     Who both were so clever
     Folks cried "Well we never,
   If they're not more old fashion'd than granny."

MAR. *(singing)*. There once was a hobbledehoy,
 Who all his spare time did employ,
  In the silly endeavour,
  To prove a youth ever
 Is a man when he isn't a boy.

NED. Who couldn't say her task the other day?
MAR. Whom did the teacher not let out to play?
NED. Who didn't know that c-a-t spells *puss?*
FAN. Who thinks he's clever?
NED. Don't make such a fuss,
 Or p'r'aps I'll take the *weasles*,
 And, sure, I dont want these ills.
ANN. B'udder Neddy's quite a poet,
MAR. O yez, O yez, O yez, we know it.
FAN. *(unrolling a paper)*. And here's his latest poem ;
 Grave Signior, shall I show 'em?
NED.   O ! please yourself.

FAN. *(reads)*.   "The Fairy Elf."

 A little maid once left her home,
 And 'mid the woods and fields did roam :
 All day she gathered pretty flowers,
 All night she slept in fairy bowers,
 And often such strange sights did see
 With wonder quite dumb-struck was she.

One eve, howe'er, a fairy came
To her, and 'dressed her by her name,
And said she must at once go home,
Or she would be changed to a gnome ;
And so o'ercome was she with dread
She woke, and found herself—in bed.

MAR. Well done, dear Ned, a really clever rhyme,
FAN. Last verse ridiculous : the first sublime.

(A bell is heard ringing.)

MAR. But there's the bell, it now is dinner time.

[*Exeunt omnes shouting* " *Hurrah, hurrah.*"]

POLLY AND HER PONY.

Many, many years ago
I a little maid did know,
Fair she was as new-fall'n snow—
    Fair and young :
And a pony she possess'd,
Which, of course, she deemed earth's best,
And, in praise of it, with zest
    This song sung :—

" Nim-a-nim-a-nim-a-nack,
Seated on a pony's back,
Is it possible to lack
    Pride or pleasure?
For my part I think it's not,
For a pony I have got,
And to see how he can trot
    'S worth a treasure.

I have had him quite two years,
And he neither kicks nor rears,
As, devoid of foolish fears,
        Him I mount ;
And a-nim-a-nim-a-nack,
Gallop gaily on his back,
With glad clicks-a-click-a-clack
        You might count.

Oh ! I love my pony Loo,
And my pony loves me, too,
Friends indeed we are and true—
        Lovers e'en :
And the whip I never crack
O'er his pretty spotted back,
But go nim-a-nim-a-nack
        Like a queen."

O! SPEAK A KIND WORD WHEN YOU CAN.

O ! speak a kind word when you can,
  As you traverse Life's valley of tears ;
For the sorrows allotted to man
  Increase, beyond doubt, with his years :
And his heart oft is wasted with pain,
  And his face oft is woe-worn and wan ;
Then—to comfort both bosom and brain—
  O! speak a kind word when you can.

O ! speak a kind word when you can,
  For the ills that their fellows must bear
None can know, tho' the whole world they scan
  With the strictest and minutest care.
Its anguish from others to hide,
  Not unseldom seems misery's plan ;
Then—whilst upon earth you abide—
  O ! speak a kind word when you can.

O ! speak a kind word when you can,
   Kind words you will get in return,
For whene'er Friendship's flame any fan,
   For them soon does Love's fire burn ;
And when you the borders have cross'd
   Of Life's valley—and brief is its span—
You will find not a syllable lost,
   O ! speak a kind word when you can.

ANNA AND ANN.

Anna and Ann are two dear little girls—
                    Darling girls—
                    Bright as pearls
Are their bonnie blue een, and their curls
Over their shoulders the wind waves and whirls—
                    Tosses and twirls,
                    Up and down hurls,
Like streamers the sailor masthead-high unfurls:
Yes Anna and Ann are two dear little girls—
                    Winsome girls.

Ann is a maiden whose years are but three—
                    Only three,
                    Yet is she
In childhood's lore learned as learned can be ;
Her tongue rarely rests for a second, yet we,
                    From weariness free,
                    Listen with glee
To her unending flow of phil-os-o-phy,
For Ann is a maiden whose years are but three—
                    Merely three.

Anna's a damsel almost six years old—

Twice as old,

" Good as gold,"

And a fairer than she did earth never behold ;

By her charms in Life's trials are many consoled,

Yet them to unfold

No poet so bold

Has e'er proved, too well knowing their number's untold

For Anna's a damsel almost six years old—

O ! how old !

A DONKEY YCLEPT NED.

A donkey dwelt in an old farmstead—
A donkey whom people sometimes called Ned—
  But very few friends had he,
For not many could bear the unmusical bray
To which he gave vent at all hours of the day,
For the simple purpose, as I have heard say,
  Of hearing the piggies cry *Wee, wee, wee,*
  And the cocks and hens, in harmony,
Go screeching about *Cluck, cluck,*
And *Quack, quack, quack* every duck.

Whene'er he began, the farmer's wife—
Who, the farmer affirmed, was too fond of strife—
Rushed into the yard with a long-bladed knife,
And threatened at once to deprive him of life,
  For a very bad temper had she :
        And a donkey's bray,
        And a horse's neigh,

And the bellow of cows
Did her arouse,
As well as the piggies' *Wee, wee,*
And the cocks and hens' *Cluck, cluck,*
And the *Quack, quack, quack* of a duck.

But what did the donkey care?—
He fed on the freshest of fare,
And was rarely afraid
Of the threats that she made,
For her son on his back rode to school,
And to run to his aid
When the knife she display'd
Was with him an unbreakable rule :
As merry a fellow was he
As any we're likely to see,
E'en if for a week
We his compeer did seek,
And his sides he would shake in his glee
When the donkey began to bray,
In its own most unmusical way,
To hear the young piggies cry *Wee, wee, wee,*
And the cocks and hens, in harmony,
Go screeching about *Cluck, cluck,*
And *Quack, quack, quack* every duck.

The end of the donkey was sad,

Though his death made his enemies glad :

    On a cold winter's day,

    When snow on the ground lay,

    As *Hee-haw* he did bray,

    In tones gruff but gay,

    His great powers to display

    Of beginning a fray,

    A blood-vessel gave way,

    And I'm sorry to say

That the piggies, delighted, cried *Wee, wee, wee,*

And the cocks and hens, in harmony,

    Went screeching about *Cluck, cluck,*

    And *Quack, quack, quack* every duck.

ENIGMA.

PROEM.

Myself a man, by man I am chastised,
   Yet in all households ever find a place,
   And, e'en in winter-time, the meadows grace :
Death's enemy, for slaughter's self devised ;
Alike by warrior and by matron prized,
   The friend and foe of the whole human race :
A fop, a beau, in lowly guise I dwell—
Like hermit, often, in a dark and narrow cell.

I.

War rages rampant ; loud the cannon roar,
   And loud the bugles sound their shrilly call,
   To conquest or to death inciting all ;
The rivulets, in shame, run red with gore,
That clear as crystal flowed the day before ;
   And, fierce as very fiends, men fighting fall—
By me, perhaps, struck down in manhood's prime,
And sent to face their God before their natural time.

II.

The fight is o'er, the battle lost and won,
   Yet sad it is to hear the hollow moan
   Of dying men—the deep-drawn curse or groan
Of half an army, see the havoc done
By bloody carnage, as the setting sun—
   A blush of horror o'er its brightness thrown—
Sinks slowly in the west, tho', with my aid,
Do doctors strive to save the wrecks that War has made.

III.

Again has Peace her spotless flag unfurl'd,
   And men in fellowship clasp hand in hand ;
   Again does Commerce land unite with land,
And sweet security waft o'er the world :
Again the bolts of warfare rust unhurl'd,
   And dire destruction is no longer plann'd :
'Tis summertime, and in the fields I rear
My humble head to tell that harvest-tide is near.

IV.

Bronzed Autumn comes, with golden hues o'ercast,
   And countless tints of fast-decaying leaves ;
   The corn is cut, and stands in stooks and sheaves,
Dispelling fear of winter—till at last

D

Into the garner gathered—once more pass'd
  The harvest, like a dream that Fancy weaves :
The farmer makes his men a merry feast
At which the part I play is by no means the least.

V.

Christmas approaches, and men's souls are fill'd
  With gladness at the thought of coming cheer ;
  What reck Mankind that Nature's dull or drear,
Or north-winds blow, or finger-tips are chill'd ?—
Into the heart is heavenly love instill'd,
  And glorious tidings fall upon the ear :—
" Peace and goodwill :" still I am sometimes seen,
As in the summer, deck'd in fairy robes of green.

VI.

'Tis New Year's Day, and blithely ring the bells
  A welcome to the new-born babe ; glad shouts
  Blend with the strains and silence all our doubts
Of future bliss ; the heart all gloom dispels ;
And, Hope-exalted, high the bosom swells :
  Yet some, alas ! in wild tumultuous routs
Their feelings vent—of these, 'tis sometimes said
That I am chief :—so charged I can but bow my head.

MY FIRST JOURNEY IN THE TRAIN.

I remember, I remember,
  When aught touches Memory's springs,
With what pleasure I look'd forward,
  Borne on Hope's exultant wings,
To the time that day by day drew near—
  Tho' oft did I complain
Of its slow approach—when I should take
  My first journey in the train.

I remember, I remember,
  How afraid I was at first,
As the screeching locomotive
  Right into the station burst ;
How, at last, into a carriage
  Jump'd I, tho' to stay out fain—
Wishing to postpone a few more hours
  My first journey in the train.

I remember, I remember,
  As along we speeding went,
How my fears all vanish'd, and I grew
  Too eager and intent
In watching how the woods and fields
  Went round and round again,
To think of aught else, as I took
  My first journey in the train.

I remember, I remember,
  When we reach'd of it the end
How I thought that on the railroad I
  My days should like to spend ;
How, as I alighted, that my heart
  Was fraught with woe and pain,
And Life's happiness seem'd over with
  My first journey in the train.

MATILDA DE JONES.

Matilda de Jones was an ill-tempered girl,
To whatever you said she replied, like a churl,
With a curl
   Of her upper lip :
So, of course, no one loved Miss Matilda de Jones,
And wherever she went she was greeted with groans,
Loud as the moans
   On a sinking ship.

It pains me, moreo'er, that I cannot record
That by old or by young she ever was heard
To speak a kind word,
   Or look cheerful and bright ;
All, alas ! I can state is she lived a sad life,
As all people do whose existence is rife
With snarling and strife,
   Morn, noon, and night.

If you said it was warm, she would answer, Oh, no!
She couldn't imagine what made you think so,
Fit for snow
   Was the weather *she* wot :
But hint it was cold, she would grant it *might* be,
Yet as warm as a piece of new toast was she,
At breakfast or tea
   All smoking and hot.

If you started to sing she declared that a *riot*
Ever made her head ache—e'en tho' you could deny it—
And so, still and quiet
   You had to remain :
But if you yourself with a lark on the wing
Did not care to compete, *she* was certain to sing,
And make the walls ring
   Again and again.

Like the Miller of Dee, that the song tells us of,
Very selfish was she, and nobody did love,
Below or above,
   Save Matilda de Jones ;
So the consequence was that nobody she saw
For Matilda de Jones cared a single straw,
Or listened with awe
   To her dissonant tones.

So whatever you do, little boys and girls,
Beware of being ill-tempered churls,
And disgracing with curls
   The upper lip :
Or else, I'm afraid, like Matilda de Jones,
Wherever you go you'll be greeted with groans,
Loud as the moans
   On a sinking ship.

PLAY WHILE YOU MAY.

I love to hear the joyful shouts,
And watch the wild bewildering routs,
    Of boys and girls at play :
For then I know Life's morning light
Is not obscured by clouds of night,
And all things still seem fair and bright,
    And hearts beat blithe and gay.

Play on, dear children, while you may,
With merry games keep care away
    As long as e'er you can :
Let future woe not make you dumb,
Think not of sorrows yet to come ;
Too soon, alas ! will they benumb,
    Too soon each face be wan.

Play, boys and girls, with might and main,
For childhood ne'er will come again,
    Nor e'er its guileless mirth :
Join, every one, the happy band
Of those who voice and chest expand,
Shame on you all who listless stand,
    Or mope about the hearth !

BOBBY'S FIRST SUIT.

Little Bobby now is
    Quite a man, I trow ;
Do you not see how his
    Arms swing to and fro :
How he holds his head up
    Like a hero bold
To his death-doom led up
    In the days of old :
How he seems oppress'd in
    A reclining pose ?—
Little Bobby's dress'd in
    His first suit of clothes !

Look how Bobby marches,
    Soldierly and slow,
Stately as the larches
    That in wild-woods grow ;
How he feels each pocket,
    Empty tho' it be—

Yet that some may mock it
  Half-afraid is he :
Powerless to rest in
  A reclining pose,
Little Bobby's dress'd in
  His first suit of clothes !

Bravo, little Bobby !
  May you never ride
A less virtuous hobby
  Than you now bestride :
May your strivings ever
  Be as wanting guile,
And in each endeavour
  Success on you smile !
Finding naught of zest in
  A reclining pose,
Little Bobby's dress'd in
  His first suit of clothes.

LEARN YOUR LESSONS.

Learn your lessons, boys and girls,
  With a right good will,
For the time, you'll find, will come
  When you'll wish that still
You were hard at work in school
Conning, e'en, some ruesome rule.

Learn your lessons, boys and girls,
  While you've yet the chance ;
All your knowledge you will need
  If you would *advance*
In the paths of toil and strife
Which appear in after life.

Learn your lessons, boys and girls,
  Show what you can do :
Father, mother, both are glad
  When they know that you
Never leave your tasks undone,
For but thus success is won.

CHARADE.

To virtue and valour *my first* is awarded,
And by most of mortals with longing regarded ;
A recompense 'tis to integrity ever,
However successful to artifice never ;
The roguish and vicious affect to despise it,
The upright and honest 'bove all things else prize it.

My second is not in all persons' possession,
Altho' of their want few to men make confession ;
Yet legion are they who believe they possess it,
Nay, more, have it not, tho' they boldly profess it ;
But whether or not of this fact they have knowledge
A question, in sooth, is to puzzle a college.

My whole is by many pursued with persistence
As the *summum bonum* of earthly existence ;
Yet cynics aver that to ride in a carriage,
And thereby have license poor folks to disparage,
Is all it amounts to 'mongst civilized people,
For which wicked thought they each night ought to sleep
   ill.

THE LITTLE DRUMMER.

I am only a little drummer,
  A little drummer-boy,
Tum-a-tum-tum, tum-a-tum-tum,
Yet each day of my life is filled
  To overflow with joy,
  Tum-a-tum-tum-tum-tum-tum.

A soldier's uniform is mine,
  Its colour a scarlet red,
Tum-a-tum-tum, tum-a-tum-tum,
And a snow-white feather flutters
  In the breeze above my head,
  Tum-a-tum-tum-tum-tum-tum.

I rouse the tired and weary
  With the beating of my drum,
Tum-a-tum-tum, tum-a-tum-tum,

For they know when they hear its warning
    'Tis time to drill to come,
    Tum-a-tum-tum-tum-tum.

My father was a soldier—
    A soldier staunch and true,
Tum-a-tum-tum, tum-a-tum-tum,
And died for his King and his Country,
    As I am willing to do,
    Tum-a-tum-tum-tum-tum.

My mother's a soldier's daughter,
    As gentle as she is brave,
Tum-a-tum-tum, tum-a-tum-tum,
And oft on the battle-field death has faced
    The dying and wounded to save,
    Tum-a-tum-tum-tum-tum.

And she loveth her little drummer
    With a twofold motherly love,
Tum-a-tum-tum, tum-a-tum-tum,
For the sake of himself, and his father's sake,
    At rest now in realms above,
    Tum-a-tum-tum-tum-tum.

Yes, she loveth her little drummer,
    And never a day goes by,
Tum-a-tum-tum, tum-a-tum-tum,
But she prayeth that he like a soldier
    May live and be ready to die.
    Tum-a-tum-tum-tum-tum,
    Tum-a-tum-tum-tum-tum.

YES AND NO.

Sometimes it is right to say Yes,
  Sometimes it is right to say No,
Then ought we—as all little folks will confess—
  Much care on their use to bestow.

If tempted to say a cross word,
  Or sign of ill-nature to show,
'Tis our duty, as soon as the Tempter is heard,
  To answer courageously No.

But if we see sorrow or grief,
  Or aught that the heart doth oppress,
Before we are orally asked for relief
  Unconsciously should we say Yes.

Tho' we are inclined to say Yes
  When we feel 'twould be wrong to do so,
The voice of our conscience should we ne'er suppress,
  But without hesitation say No.

E

Or if to say No we incline,
　And our soul no assent doth express,
Undoubtedly is the omission divine,
　And most willingly should we say Yes.

Sometimes it is right to say Yes,
　Sometimes it is right to say No,
Then ought we—as all little folks will confess—
　Much care on their use to bestow.

LITTLE WILLIE DAVIS.

Little Willie Davis
    Is the funniest fellow out,
There's nothing underneath the sky
    He doesn't talk about ;
He prattles and he chatters
    From the moment he awakes
Till the moment into Dreamland he
    His nightly journey takes ;
And he asks the queerest questions
    Human ears have ever heard—
Not unseldom not a listener
    Can answer him a word.
        Little Willie Davis
            Is the funniest fellow out,
        There's nothing underneath the sky
            He doesn't talk about.

He wonders why he loves mamma,
  And why mamma loves him,
And why his auntie Emily
  So slender is and slim ;
He wonders why to school he's forced
  To go, day after day,
When the shining sun invites him
  Over hill and dale to stray ;
He wonders if the stars are holes
  Through which God sees us all,
And he wonders where the clouds came from
  Out of which the snowflakes fall.
        Little Willie Davis .
          Is the funniest fellow out,
          There's nothing underneath the sky
          He doesn't talk about.

Yet his father and his mother
  Of his gossip never tire,
For to them his voice sounds sweeter
  Than the music of the lyre ;
And they do their very utmost
  To supply his endless wants,
In which task they're oft assisted
  By his uncles and his aunts ;

For they all love little Willie
  And his guileless, winning ways,
And believe that wisdom may be found
  In everything he says.
        Little Willie Davis
          Is the funniest fellow out,
        There's nothing underneath the sky
          He doesn't talk about.

THE COW THAT COUGHED.

A cow had a cough, a cough oh ! so bad
That never before a cow such a cough had ;
It coughed all the day, and it coughed all the night,
It coughed in the dark, and it coughed in the light,
And it made all its fellow-cows stick out their tails,
And to see its distress fill the air with loud wails.

When the maid went to milk it her heart sore did ache,
For in fear that the cow choked to death she did quake ;
But her sorrow to anger was suddenly turned,
And her cheeks in her rage like the setting sun burned ;
For the cow with its coughing knocked over the pail,
And lashed the maid right o'er her face with its tail.

The farmer grew anxious about the cow's life,
And said in the mournfullest tones to his wife,
" I had better set off for the doctor with haste—
If the cow we would save we have no time to waste :"
So he mounted his roan, and away galloped he
Far faster than swallows hie over the sea.

He brought back the doctor, the doctor looked wise,
And first rubbed his nose, and next winked his eyes,

And then shook his head as if wanting it off,
And listened quite solemnly to the cow's cough ;
Then its pulse he did feel, and declared that he thought
That the cow he could cure, as a good doctor ought.

But alas and alack ! when they wanted the cow
Its medicine to take, it bellowed "Not now,"
And to get it to take it they could not succeed—
The cow to their entreaties would not pay heed ;
So the consequence was, as I needn't rehearse,
The animal gradually got worse and worse.

Then they tried severe measures, and over its back
With a big gibby stick came down fiercely whack, whack,
And though there's no doubt that the poor beast they
    pained,
Yet foolishly stubborn through all it remained,
And would not partake of a single wee drop
Of what down its throat they were anxious to pop.

At last it became so worn out and so weak,
That the farmer again had the doctor to seek,
But still it refused—though with pain it did shake—
The medicine the doctor decreed it to take ;
So despite all his efforts, and all that he tried,
It coughed and it coughed, it coughed and—it died.

HURRAH FOR HOLIDAY-TIME.

Hurrah for Holiday-time,
  With its freedom from home-task and school :
Books banished—Life's prose turned to rhyme—
Hurrah for Holiday-time !—
E'en dominies deem cram a crime,
  And to study against the rule :
Hurrah for Holiday-time,
  With its freedom from home-task and school.

WASHINGTON AND THE AXE.

George Washington's father
　　Once gave him an axe,
And soon was George ready
　　Its keen edge to tax ;
So into the garden
　　Delighted sped he,
And chopped all to pieces
　　A young cherry tree.

Ere long George's father
　　The damage did spy,
And asked George about it—
　　Did George, think you, try
To deceive his kind father ?
　　O ! hear his reply :—
"I did it, dear father ;
　　I can't tell a lie."

Like George, little children,
  The truth always speak,
For cowards in Falsehood
  Alone refuge seek :
Be upright and downright,
  And—heads held up high—
Like George say, when tempted,
  "We can't tell a lie."

THREE SONNETS.

I.

YESTERDAY.

Christ's natal day draws nigh—the day whereon
  Man most commiserates his fellows' woes,
  And holier bliss enjoys by helping those
In tribulation : troubles, every one,
By sufferers forgotten—pain's pangs gone
  For a brief space—a roseate hue Life shows
  To sorrowing mortals, something doth disclose
That makes it worth the living : dull are none.

None, say I, none?—therein I err, for some
  There are that murmur and repine because—
Contrary to his custom of old time,
  And right succession of the natural laws—
  In garb of green doth Father Christmas come
Ours, grumble they, is not an Austral clime.

II.

TO-DAY.

To-day in blinding gusts North-Easters blow,
    To-day in white robes are the house-tops clad,
    And I, who erstwhile seemed a little sad
At the approach of Christmas without snow,
Feel not my cheeks reflect the ruddy glow
    Of healthful happiness—nor even am glad
    That soon on frozen streams shall it be had,
Since " seasonable weather" now we know.

Wrapped up in sables and in furs I sped,
    This morn, thro' the deserted streets, and felt—
Despite my over-clothes—the bitter cold ;
And, as I hurried onwards,—faint, half dead,
    Crouched on a doorway from the hailstones' pelt,
A woman with a babe did I behold.

III.

FOR-EVER.

Loud roared the wind, fast fell the stony shower
  With thuds on wall and pavement—such a day
  Was it as men shield dogs on : yet there lay
The woman with her babe—bereft of power
To move a further yard, nay, but to cower
  Against the sheltering railings : I did stay
  My footsteps, and—but all in vain—essay
To rouse her—Death came unto both that hour.

No more the raging storms 'gainst her will beat ;
  No more will frosts benumb ; no more, no more
  Will heaviness o'ertake her weary feet ;
And never more—forgetful of the poor,
And all the evils that they must endure—
  Shall I "the winters of old time" long for.

FORGIVE AND FORGET.

'Tis the best of all rules—
    As oft-times is sung—
For wise folk *and* fools,
    For old *and* for young,
As they journey thro' life,
    Whene'er insult is met,
To think not of strife,
    But forgive and forget.

If some one has spoken
    To you a cross word,
Oh ! give not a token
    That it you have heard :
'Tis better by far
    An example to set
Of peace than of war,
    And forgive and forget.

For blows return kisses
  Whenever you can,
For know you that this is
  The only true plan
By which to gain Heaven :
  As you hope *your* debt
In the future forgiven,
  Forgive and forget.

THE FOOLISH GOSLINGS.

'Twas nigh Michaelmas time, and a stately old goose,
  That had seen, I believe, thirteen summers,
Yet whose coat was still white as a new flag of truce,
  Thus harangued a lot of late-comers ;
A lot of late-comers, perhaps I should state,
  Both into the world and the farmyard,
Where she had herself all her life dwelt elate,
  And reckoned it naught but a calm yard.

" My sweet little dears, I am happy to see
  The smiles of your innocent faces,
And hope most sincerely they never may be
  Exchanged for a sufferer's grimaces :
And yet should you scorn my advice, dears, to take,
  Or deign not to me now to hearken,
Very soon, I'm afraid, this exchange you will make,
  And not long with your shadows earth darken.

" For the next week or two you'll be fed on the fat
 Of the land, and have all sorts of dainties ;
But like wise little goslings be careful of what
 You devour, for man's way often quaint is ;
He'll feed you and feast you on toothsomest fare—
 Minced meats, and bran mashes, and barley,
And when you are plump as the maddest March hare
 Will slay you without further parley.

" For this is the season he fancies goose-flesh
 Most digestible and most delicious ;
So heed what I say, and beware of the mesh
 He is weaving around you so vicious :
Refuse to partake of the food that he fain
 Would have you be eating all day, dears ;
Ay, eat not nor drink till each rivals a cane
 In its thinness, or e'en a sun's ray, dears."

When she ceased, the pleased goslings applauded her
 speech,
 And cried they would do as she taught them,
But alas—just as folks practise not what they preach—
 To obey her they never bethought them :
They ate and they ate of whate'er they could get,
 And of guzzling ne'er proved themselves shirkers ;
They ate and they ate all that for them was set,
 Till they all became fat as prize porkers.

F

Then—sad to relate—*then* the farmer declared
   Every one of them ready for killing,
And not in the least for their groans and moans cared,
   For his coffers required re-filling :
IIe twisted their necks, though they screeched and they
   screamed,
   And bewailed they'd not kept themselves thinner.

    *   *   *   *   *   *

The moral is plain, or by me so is deemed,
   Who helped to eat one cooked for dinner.

THE END.

DERBY AND NOTTINGHAM : FRANK MURRAY.